* *For Emma* *
♥

TRANSWORLD PUBLISHERS LTD
61-63 Uxbridge Road, London W5 5SA

15-25 Helles Avenue, Moorebank, NSW 2170

3 William Pickering Drive, Albany, Auckland

DOUBLEDAY CANADA LTD
105 Bond Street, Toronto, Ontario M5B 1Y3

Published 1995 by Doubleday
a division of Transworld Publishers Ltd
Designed by Ian Butterworth

A catalogue record for this book is available
from the British Library

ISBN 0 385 405707

Printed in Belgium by Proost

The OWL and the PUSSY-CAT

E D W A R D   L E A R

Illustrated by

I A N   B E C K

DOUBLEDAY

London New York Toronto Sydney Auckland

The Owl and the Pussy-cat went to sea

In a beautiful pea-green boat,

They took some honey,

and plenty of money,

Wrapped up in a five-pound note.

The Owl looked up to the stars above,
And sang to a small guitar,

"O lovely Pussy! O Pussy my love,
   What a beautiful Pussy you are,
         You are,
            You are!
         What a beautiful Pussy you are!"

Pussy said to the Owl, "You elegant fowl!
How charmingly sweet you sing!

O let us be married! Too long we have tarried:
But what shall we do for a ring?"

January

February

May

June

September

October

They sailed away, for a year and a day

march

April

July

August

November

December

To the land where the Bong-tree grows

And there in a wood a Piggy-wig stood

With a ring at the end of his nose,
His nose,
His nose,
With a ring at the end of his nose.

"Dear Pig, are you willing to sell for one shilling

Your ring?" Said the Piggy, "I will."

So they took it away, and were married next day

By the Turkey who lives on the hill.

They dined on mince,

and slices of quince,

Which they ate with a runcible spoon;

And hand in hand, on the edge of the sand,

They danced by the light of the moon,

The moon,
The moon,

They danced by the light of the moon.